This Little Tiger book belongs to:

_____

_____

_____

For Matthew
~ CL

For Sven
~ GH

LITTLE TIGER PRESS
1 The Coda Centre, 189 Munster Road, London SW6 6AW
www.littletiger.co.uk

First published in Great Britain 2003
This edition published 2016

ISBN 978-1-84869-474-3
Printed in China
LTP/1900/1573/0616

1 3 5 7 9 10 8 6 4 2

MOLLY and the STORM

Christine Leeson   Gaby Hansen

LITTLE TIGER PRESS
London

It was the first sunny day after weeks and
weeks of rain.
"Can we go out to play, Mum?" asked Molly
Mouse, dancing in the pale sunshine. "Please?"
"So long as you keep an eye on the weather,"
said Mother Mouse.
"I'm sure more rain is on the way."

Molly and her brothers
and sister scampered across
the fields. They chased each other round
hawthorn trees, frothing white with blossom.

They hopped through
carpets of bluebells.

They were enjoying themselves
so much that they didn't notice
it was suddenly getting darker.

A large drop of rain fell on Molly's
nose – and another, and then another.
Big black clouds filled the sky, and
the rain started to fall faster and faster.
"We'll never get home in time," groaned Molly.
"Where can we shelter until it stops?"

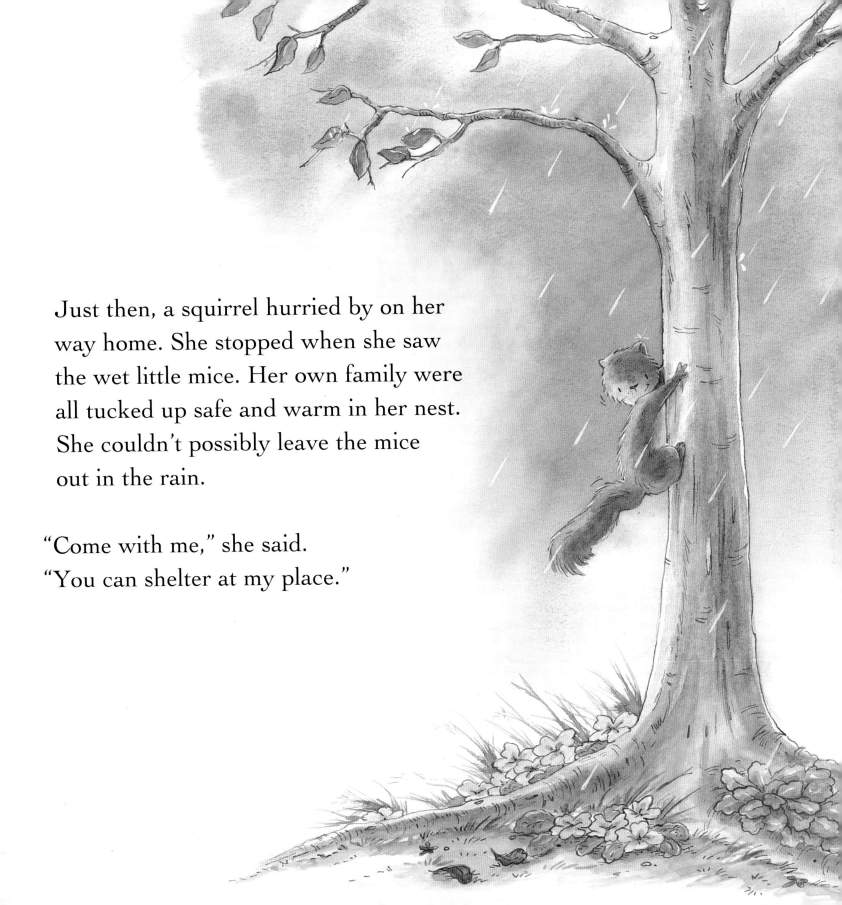

Just then, a squirrel hurried by on her
way home. She stopped when she saw
the wet little mice. Her own family were
all tucked up safe and warm in her nest.
She couldn't possibly leave the mice
out in the rain.

"Come with me," she said.
"You can shelter at my place."

Squirrel ran ahead and bounded
up a tree, but the mice didn't follow.
"Your house is too high and it doesn't
look safe in this storm," sighed Molly.

An old harvest mouse popped
her head out from under some leaves.
"You can stay with me," she said kindly,
"I have a nice warm nest of twigs."

Harvest Mouse scuttled to her home, but
the mice didn't follow. They could see that
her woven nest was far too small for them all.

"You can come to our place," cried a little rabbit,
"and join my baby brothers and sisters in the
warmth of our burrow." She couldn't leave
these poor little mice out in the storm.

Rabbit popped down the rabbit hole, but the
mice stayed outside. "Your home is very full,"
said Molly, peering inside at all the baby rabbits.
"I think we'd all be too squashed."

Before Rabbit had time to answer, they both
heard someone calling. Molly pricked her ears.
"It's Mother Mouse!" she squeaked.

"Thank goodness I've found you!" cried Mother
Mouse. "The storm is getting worse. But
there's an old hollow oak tree
nearby where we can shelter
until the rain stops."

The hollow oak tree stood at the top of a slope. The mice
scrambled inside and were soon warm and dry.
"We'll stay here tonight," said Mother Mouse. "You can
all curl up together and go to sleep."

But Molly couldn't sleep. She lay listening to the roar
of the wind and the lashing of the rain, and she was
worried about her new friends. Would Harvest Mouse's
home be destroyed? Surely Rabbit's burrow would be
flooded, and Squirrel's nest blown away? Molly looked
at her family, sleeping snugly. She couldn't leave her
friends out in the storm.

Molly hurried outside. The wind tugged and
pulled at her as she struggled across the field.
There, huddled under a swaying tree,
was Squirrel.

"You must come with me,"
said Molly. "We've found
the perfect shelter."

Just then, looking tired and bedraggled,
the old harvest mouse appeared out of
the grass.
"Can I come too?" she asked.
"Of course," said Molly.

As they made their way
back, they passed Rabbit
and her family huddled
under a hedge. "You'll
be nice and warm if
you come with us,"
said Molly.

At last Molly and her new friends reached the shelter of the old oak tree. Outside, the wind battered the trees and flattened the grasses. But inside, everyone was safe and dry.

The wind had dropped by the time morning came, and as the sun crept up into the sky the friends crawled out of their burrow. There before them was a rainbow, stretching as far as the eye could see.

"It's for you, Molly," whispered the old harvest mouse. "It's a special present for saving us."
And Molly smiled happily, surrounded by her family and all her new friends.